2/97

APACHE RODEO

Library of Congress Cataloging-in-Publication Data

Hoyt-Goldsmith, Diane
    Apache rodeo / Diane Hoyt-Goldsmith : photographs by Lawrence
  Migdale. -- 1st ed.
        p.   cm.
      Includes index.
      ISBN 0-8234-1164-8
      1. Apache Indians--Juvenile literature. 2. Rodeos--Arizona-
  -Juvenile literature.   I. Migdale, Lawrence.   II. Title.
  E99.A6H795 1995
  973' .04972--dc20   94-26583
                                                       CIP
                                                       AC

Acknowledgments

    This book would not have been possible without the friendship and cooperation of some very special people. We would like to thank Rubert and Jo Ann Lupe and their children, Felecita, Skyler, Elias, and Jace, for opening their home to us and sharing their experiences before, during, and after the White Mountain Apache Fair and Rodeo.

    We appreciate the friendship and cooperation of their families: Gertie and Roger Lupe; Fitzgerald, Eliza, Frankie, and Mathias Lupe; Ignatius, Cheryl, and Lillian Kay Lupe; Roger Lupe, Jr., Emil Lupe, and Phil Lupe. Mary Lou, Guy, and Erick Benally were especially helpful and we appreciate their participation in shaping this book.

    We send thanks to the White Mountain Apache Tribal Chairman, Ronnie Lupe; to Roger Leslie and the Fair and Rodeo committee; to Myrna Gunther Hillyard, Principal of the Whiteriver Elementary School; and to stockman, Caspar Baca and Cody, the bravest rodeo clown we have ever met. We appreciate the help of Hugh Lee and Lester Buck of the Fort Apache Timber Company (FATCO), and thanks to Deloria Lee for her help. Thanks also to Kenny Black for his participation.

    Eva Watts, who gave of her time and experience, taught us much about the Apache way of life, both then and now. Her life is a treasury of traditions, and we thank her for sharing them generously with us. Linda Kay Holden gave us many suggestions on the manuscript and we appreciate her guidance.

    As always, we appreciate the talents of Lorna Mason, who brings to her contributions the concerns and insights of a historian. We thank our wonderful editor, Margery Cuyler, for her advice, enthusiasm, and inspiration.

    Finally, a very special thanks is due to Ed Burnam, for introducing us to the Lupe family, and for his careful reading of the manuscript. We appreciate permission to photograph a burden basket from his collection, made by Melissa Gregg of Whiteriver, Arizona.

    For those who wish to experience the White Mountain Apache Tribal Fair and Rodeo, please write or call for more information.
    White Mountain Apache
    Tribal Fair and Rodeo Commission
    P.O. Box 1709
    Whiteriver, AZ 85941
    (602) 338-4621

APACHE RODEO

BY DIANE HOYT-GOLDSMITH

PHOTOGRAPHS BY LAWRENCE MIGDALE

HOLIDAY HOUSE - NEW YORK

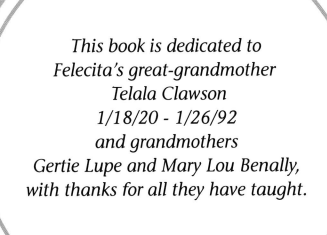

*This book is dedicated to
Felecita's great-grandmother
Telala Clawson
1/18/20 - 1/26/92
and grandmothers
Gertie Lupe and Mary Lou Benally,
with thanks for all they have taught.*

Felecita sits on the banks of the White River. She is wearing an Apache camp dress and a special beaded necklace made by her grandmother, Mary Lou. Felecita's Apache name, Ish'ka'łii (ISH-kah-GLEE) was given to her by her grandmother, Gertie. She was named for a beautiful and kind person, full of smiles and happiness. Gertie tells Felecita that all the Apache people used to be that way. But it is not like that anymore and that is why Felecita was given this name.

My name is Felecita (*FIL-ah-CEE-tah*) La Rose. I live on the Fort Apache Indian Reservation in Whiteriver, Arizona. I have lived here all my life. I am lucky to grow up in such a special place.

5

The road to Whiteriver climbs up from the desert and passes through Salt River Canyon. The plateau above is dotted with pine and spruce trees.

Whiteriver is the home of the White Mountain Apaches, one of the five groups of Western Apaches. It is located in a beautiful valley on a plateau in eastern Arizona. The town is named for the White River that flows through it. Nearby you can see the peaks of the White Mountains. The White Mountain Apaches have lived in the shadow of these sacred mountains for more than three centuries.

I live with my mother, father, and three younger brothers, Skyler, Elias, and Jace. Our house is next door to the elementary school in town.

I am ten years old and in the fifth grade. Although everyone speaks English at school, many children speak Apache at home with their parents and grandparents.

Apache is an Athapaskan language that is similar to the languages spoken by people far to the north in Alaska and Canada. The languages are alike because the Apaches began to migrate south from the arctic regions around a thousand years ago.

In school, I enjoy learning about the history of my people. Although the way we live today is very different from the way the Apaches lived in the past, we still follow many of the old traditions.

(Left) Houses in Whiteriver usually include corrals and barns for livestock. Most people own cattle and a few horses.

(Right) Nine hundred students attend Felecita's elementary school. The school buildings are modern and have up-to-date technology. There are computers in the library, but Felecita still likes books.

Because of their nomadic way of life, the Apaches owned few possessions. They produced very little pottery but they made baskets that were light and useful. The Apaches made a basket jug called a *tus* that could be used to carry water. By rubbing piñon pitch on the sides, they made it watertight. The Apaches are still making beautiful baskets. This burden basket is just like the ones that Apaches have used for hundreds of years to carry things from place to place.

Long ago, the Apaches were nomads. They traveled from one place to another, collecting wild foods to eat. Women gathered plants, berries, and nuts. They also planted a few crops. Men hunted the deer and elk that lived in the forests and mountains.

In the 1500s, many different Apache bands were living in the Southwest. The bands were usually made up of several large family groups and numbered from thirty-five to two hundred people. Sometimes the bands came together for special ceremonies or to defend themselves in times of war.

Each band picked its own leader or chief. The chief was responsible for finding animals to hunt and for locating a good place to camp. The best leader was one who could provide for his people and settle personal disputes within the band.

At first, the Apaches went everywhere on foot. Some bands, especially on the plains, used dogs to help them carry things from one camp to the next. However, when the Spanish brought horses to the New World from Europe in the 1500s, the Apaches became excellent riders. Horses made it easier for them to travel long distances.

The Apaches traded with communities throughout the Southwest. They brought buffalo hides from the prairie to the Pueblo Indians. From the Pueblos, they got cloth, metal tools, pottery, and grain.

Today we hear stories about how children in those days were raised. My father tells us that young boys ran for miles every day. After running, they plunged their sweating bodies into the freezing water of mountain streams. This training helped make them tough and strong enough to stand the hardships of their lives. Apache girls were as tough as the boys. Many girls became excellent runners and riders as well.

(Right) Most of Felecita's relatives live in Whiteriver. She helps to entertain her new cousin, Lillian Kay. Although Lillian Kay is only three months old, she already has a tiny pair of Apache moccasins.

(Left) Felecita is a member of the school track team. She trains with her grandfather, who has been a good runner all his life. Although he is sixty years old, he can still run the mile in five and a half minutes.

Felecita and Skyler like to trade basketball cards. They enjoy watching the game on television almost as much as they like shooting hoops in the backyard or playing the game with friends.

Felecita and her brothers enjoy a lunch of Indian fry bread at a roadside stand near their house.

Today the Apaches are no longer nomads. In the 1870s, the United States government built a military fort near the White River. Named Fort Apache, it became the site of a reservation for the White Mountain Apaches.

A reservation is a community established by the United States government as a place for American Indian tribes to live. When settlers from Europe first arrived in the 1600s, many groups of Native Americans were already living here. In the beginning, relations between the Europeans and the Indians were friendly. But as the numbers of Europeans grew, so did the problems. The newcomers fought the Native Americans for their land. When gold was discovered, the fighting became worse. Some Indians died defending their homes and families. Others died from smallpox and different diseases that the settlers brought from Europe.

The Native Americans who survived were soon outnumbered. Gradually their territory was taken from them and they were moved to reservations. Often, these reservations were far from their original homelands.

Fortunately the land reserved for our tribe was nearly the same territory that the White Mountain people had lived on for centuries. No gold was ever discovered here, so the White Mountain Apaches did not feel the pressure for land that other Indian tribes did.

Today there are four Apache reservations in the United States. In Arizona, Apaches live at the Fort Apache and San Carlos reservations. The Jicarilla *(hi-cah-REE-yah)* and the Mescalero *(mes-cah-LEH-roh)* Apaches live on reservations in New Mexico. Many Chiricahua *(CHI-rih-KOW-ah)* Apaches have moved there to live with the Mescaleros. Some Chiricahuas still live far away in Oklahoma, where their relatives were sent as prisoners of war in the 1890s.

Felecita, along with a friend, watches her mother work on a beadwork design. Her mother plans to sew the decorations on a new rodeo shirt she is making for Felecita's father.

(Right) Eva enjoys telling stories to the children, but only in the wintertime. In the summer, the animals might hear the stories. The Apaches believe that could bring bad luck. In winter, when the animals are sleeping, it is safe to talk about them if you speak in a soft voice.

(Left) Eva knows many traditional ways. Sometimes a friend brings her the quills from a porcupine that was killed on the highway. Eva prepares the quills to decorate buckskin clothing and moccasins.

Some of the elderly people who live in Whiteriver have heard stories from their parents and grandparents about what life was like before the reservation. Our friend Eva is eighty years old. She tells us that her parents could travel freely, hunting and camping wherever they liked.

Eva says that for her, the reservation is like a prison. Before it existed, the Apaches could go anywhere they wanted to. She doesn't think the reservation is good.

My father thinks of it in another way. He believes the reservation has helped the White Mountain Apaches to stay together. Living together as a group has helped us to keep our identity, culture, and much of our way of life from disappearing.

In my family, we like traditional Apache activities. Sometimes we go on long car trips to find good places to collect acorns for Apache stew. Although food gathering is no longer necessary for our survival, it is a lot more fun than going to the supermarket.

The land at Whiteriver provides much of what we need. If we want wood to burn in our stoves for heat, there is a place in the forest where we can cut it. There was a time when, if my father needed a new horse, he could trap one from the wild herds that live in the high meadows on the reservation. Some people still tan deer hides and sew moccasins from the leather. Many Apache women create beautiful beadwork and baskets.

But each of these special skills must be learned. They are not things that can be found in a book. We need to listen to our elders, to the people who still remember how to do things in the traditional way. This is an important part of our heritage.

Felecita and her mother spend an afternoon removing the husks from a pile of acorns. These were collected by Felecita's grandmother, Gertie, and will be ground up to use in a traditional Apache stew.

13

There are many jobs on the reservation. One of the most important is that of the chairman, or leader of the Apache reservation. Felecita and her mother visit Ronnie Lupe in his office. There is a flag decorated with the tribal seal on the wall. Ronnie Lupe has been elected chairman six times and has led the Apache community in Whiteriver for more than twenty years.

Felecita's grandmother, Mary Lou, has worked as a teacher in the Head Start program for young, preschool children for twenty-four years.

Whiteriver's major industry is logging. A worker figures out how much lumber can be cut from the huge logs that are piled up near the mill. The mill employs many Apaches like her, who live in and around Whiteriver. The mill is a big business for the tribe. It produces 100 million board feet of lumber and 30 million dollars of income a year.

Felecita's father works as the director of a vocational program that teaches young people the building trades. He shows one of his students the scale model of a house that the class will build for people on the reservation.

Horses graze in the lush pastures on the land along the river where Felecita and her family spend the summer.

Because we live on a high plateau, it is cold in the winter and we usually get lots of snow. The tribe runs a skiing resort in the mountains where we go during the winter, but summer is our favorite time of year.

Once the weather warms up, we spend all our evenings and weekends on our land. We drive to the other side of town, past the sawmill and the fairgrounds. We travel on a dirt road that runs behind a row of cottonwood trees.

At the end of this road, our land stretches across acres and acres of green. A lazy, chocolate-colored ribbon of water called the East Fork River flows along the southern boundary. My family keeps some cattle and a number of saddle horses there. My dad has built a barn and an arena where we can practice our rodeo skills.

One summer, we built a ramada (*rah-MAH-dah*) for shade. We put up four tree trunks to make a frame for the roof. Then we covered the top with branches to make a shady place where we could cook and eat. We made a few wickiups *(WIH-kee-ups)*, too. These are traditional Apache homes that use the ground for a floor and saplings covered with bear grass and brush for a dome-shaped roof.

On our land, we practice for the annual rodeo that takes place in Whiteriver at the end of the summer. During Labor Day weekend, Skyler, Elias, and I compete in the children's rodeo events. Then we watch our father and our uncles as they compete in the rodeo for grown-ups.

(Right) Working under the ramada, Felecita helps her mother make Apache bread for an outdoor meal. The dough is rolled into little balls. Then they are flattened into pancakes. After roasting near the hot coals of the campfire for a few minutes, the bread is ready to eat.

(Left) Felecita's uncle Erick is only a year older than she is. He likes to join the kids for a swim in the river. When it is really hot, the kids sometimes jump in with all their clothes on to cool off.

THE SUNRISE CEREMONY

The girl's godmother holds her hands and sways with her in a dance as the sun rises.

Covered with sacred clay, the girl dances in the harvest tipi with her godparents.

The Apache Sunrise Ceremony dates back to a hundreds of years ago, when the Apaches first called themselves the *Ndee* (in-DEH), "the People."

The Apaches believe that they are the descendants of Changing Woman, who was the mother of "the People." For the Apaches, she represents the ideal woman. Her importance in the Sunrise Ceremony echoes the value of women in Apache life.

Each summer, many Apache girls who come of age participate in the special ceremony that begins their transition from childhood to womanhood.

In the Sunrise Ceremony, the Apaches believe that the power of Changing Woman passes to the young girl for whom the ceremony is held. The Apaches believe that the girl "becomes" Changing Woman during the ceremony.

It takes many months to get ready for this special event. First, the girl's family must choose godparents from members of the community. They want people who are respected and whose lives embody the values of the Apache people.

The choice of godparents is very important because this man and woman will sponsor the girl during the ceremony. They will also teach her the traditions that will help her to behave correctly in her family and in the tribe. In addition, long after the ceremony is over, they will advise and guide the girl throughout her life. They will be like parents to her.

A traditional Sunrise Ceremony takes place over four days. To begin, there is a special dressing ceremony. The girl puts on a beautiful, handmade buckskin dress that has been blessed with special songs. She wears a white eagle feather in her hair and carries a hand-carved cane, decorated with feathers, as a symbol of the long life she will lead.

The ceremony usually takes place on the dance grounds in Whiteriver or at a camp in the mountains. Here saplings of oak, birch, pine, and juniper are used to build a harvest tipi.

During the ceremony, the girl dances for many hours as people sing and play the drums. The girl is sacred and has the power to heal. She prays for the people and the people pray for her.

At one point during the ceremony, the godmother massages

Apache Crown Dancers

the girl's body. The Apaches believe that the older woman's wisdom passes through her powerful fingers and hands to help mold the girl into a stronger person.

On the last night the Crown Dancers appear. Coming in from the east, they represent the G'aan or Mountain Spirits. The dancers get their name from elaborate sotol headdresses that they wear. They dress in kilts and carry sotol sticks shaped like swords. Their faces are covered with black masks and their bodies are painted with symbols and designs.

There are four dancers, one for each of the four directions — north, south, east, and west. The fifth dancer, called the clown, covers his body with white clay.

He is the leader and carries an instrument called a rhombus stick. As he swings it rapidly in a circle, it makes a beautiful humming sound that represents the wind. The Crown Dancers dance to ward off evil and to bless everyone in attendance.

The singers and drummers at the Sunrise Ceremony always face the east where the sun comes up each morning. Their songs are sacred to the Apaches. They tell the story of Changing Woman. Singing the songs over and over

again will help the girl to live in the Apache way.

On the last morning, the girl dances as the sun rises. Then, facing the sun, she kneels on a pile of blankets as her godfather paints her with sacred clay. He puts golden yellow tule pollen on her forehead and cheeks so that she will be able to have many children.

When the girl is covered with clay, her godfather circles among the crowd. With an eagle feather, he splashes pollen on the faces and shoulders of everyone there. These spots of bright yellow pollen are treasured signs that all the people have been blessed.

THE RODEO

Our father grew up with the rodeo. When he was a boy, he spent every spare moment learning rodeo skills. His father taught him how to rope and ride. He coached our father on the best way to tie a calf. Now our father teaches us.

Rodeo has been important to the people of Whiteriver for many, many years. The White Mountain Fair and Rodeo has been held in our town each summer since 1925. When the reservation brought an end to the Apache's nomadic way of life, raising cattle became an important way for my people to earn a living. The Apaches used their skill with horses to become excellent cowboys and ranchers.

During Whiteriver's annual summer rodeo, the town's population swells by about 25,000 people. Most of the people who attend are other Indians. The Navajo and Hopi come from reservations to the north, and the Pueblos come from the east. There are also many Apaches who visit from reservations in Arizona and New Mexico.

In Spanish, the word rodeo means "roundup." In the old days, cowboys got together each fall to round up the cattle that had been grazing all year on the range. They separated the cattle belonging to different ranchers before driving the animals to market. They roped calves and branded them. They rode wild horses to break them to the saddle. After all this hard work was finished, many of the cowboys still had enough energy left to see who was the best, the fastest, and the bravest.

Over the years, these cowboy contests that were held out on the range grew into the modern rodeos that we have today. The first rodeos were held in the 1880s in towns throughout the West.

Already Felecita's two-year-old brother, Jace, loves to sit on a horse. When he gets up in the morning, he puts on his cowboy boots before he eats breakfast. Sometimes, when the day is over, he goes to sleep wearing them.

Most of the rodeo skills that we learn are practical. The riding and roping that the cowboys do to manage the White Mountain tribe's large herd of beef cattle are also the skills they use in the rodeo. Skyler, Elias, and I are learning to rope. We have to practice a lot to get really good.

Felecita, Skyler, and Elias listen as their father explains how they should direct their horses through the barrel race.

Felecita practices the barrel race with the horse she will ride in the rodeo. The rider must make a clover leaf pattern between the barrels, coming as close as possible without touching them or turning them over. It takes horsemanship and riding skill to win.

As we practice, we are developing discipline. This, my father tells us, will help us throughout our lives. When my father was eighteen, he left the reservation to attend college. For the first time, he was surrounded by strangers. My father says the discipline, toughness, and determination he learned training for the rodeo helped him get through college successfully.

In the rodeo, it is impossible to win unless your mind and body are at their best. That's why alcohol and drugs are not allowed.

Felecita watches and listens as her uncle shows her the proper way to tie a calf's legs. Then Felecita tries it. In rodeo competition, the calf must stay tied for at least five seconds after she throws up her hands to signal she is finished.

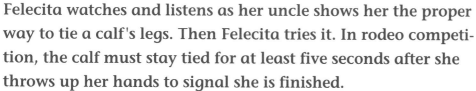

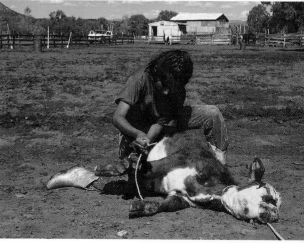

Today, a lot of Apache kids don't have much to do after school. Many of them stay at home and watch television. But we are lucky. In my family, we can always practice something new for the rodeo. We can work on roping or ride our horses. In the summer, my brothers and I are outside all the time.

(Left) Felecita's mother labels vegetables and flowers from her garden so that she can enter them in the fair.

During the week of the rodeo, there are several days when the children perform in special events. These events test the same skills that get tested in the adult rodeo. The only difference is that the animals, and children, are much smaller.

Instead of calf roping, there is goat tying. To compete in this event, I ride my horse from one end of the arena to the other. Then I jump off, grab the little goat that is tied to a pole, and throw it to the ground. As quickly as I can, I tie its legs together. When my hands go up at the end, it means I'm finished and the judges stop the clock.

Another event I compete in is the barrel race. Each contestant rides as fast as possible toward the center of the arena where three barrels are set up. The riders circle them in a clover leaf pattern, without touching the barrels or knocking them down. Then the rider races back to the starting line. The person with the best time wins.

Both Skyler and Elias like to ride calves. This is like bull riding, but on a smaller scale. Sometimes the little calves don't even want to buck, and the boys simply hang on and ride as long as they can.

(Right) Felecita's mother helps Elias get ready to ride in the children's rodeo.

(Top right) The rodeo clown is very important. The clown risks his own life and safety to make sure that the riders are not hurt.

(Top left) The rodeo clown shows Felecita and Skyler how he applies his make-up as he gets ready for the next rodeo event.

(Bottom) Skyler rides a calf and stays on for five seconds, a good time for a young cowboy.

25

THE RIDE

My father competes in calf roping and team roping, but his favorite event is riding the bulls. He likes the excitement—the thrill of riding on an animal that weighs a ton or more.

An hour before the rodeo, my father goes into the office and meets the stockman. This man travels around to rodeos in the country with his string of bucking bulls.

The stockman looks for bulls that are really "rank" and like to buck. He tries out about three hundred bulls each year. From these, he chooses about thirty to take to the rodeos. Bucking bulls are worth a great deal of money. A good rodeo bull can cost $1,500 - 4,000.

Before the bull riding begins, the stockman puts the names of the bulls into a hat. The rodeo officials draw a name for each rider. My father gets a bull called "Honky Cat." The stockman congratulates my father on getting a really "rank" bull. That means that my father will have a difficult, but high scoring ride. This is called "the luck of the draw."

Although Roger, Felecita's grandfather, no longer competes in the rodeo, he watches each event from the stands. He has been around rodeo for so long that he still has good advice to give his sons and grandchildren.

Felecita's father comes out of the gate to compete in the calf-roping event. In his teeth he carries a short rope that he will use to tie the calf's feet together.

Felecita's father pins his number onto the leg of his jeans so that the judges can easily see it. Then he straps on his spurs. The spurs will help him grip the bull with his legs. He is standing by a horse trailer that he won in a rodeo when Felecita was just a little girl.

Felecita's father goes to the corral behind the arena to look at "Honky Cat," the bull he will be riding. He wants to see how big the bull is and watch how he moves.

While the other riders in his section get ready, my father starts to think about riding the bull. He says a prayer as he thinks about the danger he will soon face.

The winner of the bull-riding contest will be the rider with the highest number of points. To qualify, the rider must stay on the bull for a full eight seconds. Then more points are given for style, for how difficult the bull is to ride, and for not touching the bull with the free hand.

An hour before the ride, my father starts to get ready. He puts on leather leg coverings called "chaps." These are partly for looks. The fringes fly in the air when the bull starts to buck. But chaps are also worn for safety. They protect the rider's legs both inside the chute and out. My father wears a pair of leather gloves to protect his hands.

There is a special bag that holds all of my father's bull riding gear. It also contains a small cross that his mother gave him, a jar of holy oil, and a tiny Bible.

To get ready, my father spends a few minutes stretching and making his body limber. He checks out his equipment, putting more rosin on the bull rope. My father doesn't watch the other riders perform. He just wants to concentrate on his ride. Then he takes time to say a prayer.

Just before his turn, my father slips into the chute and wraps the rope around the bull's chest and then winds it tightly around one hand. He gives a nod to the man holding the chute gate closed. It's time.

When the door swings open, the bull explodes into the air. My father rides for one second, then two, three, four. Each moment brings another leap, another twist, and a heavy landing. Although my father stays on the bull for five seconds, the bull finally bucks him off. He lands on the ground, too soon to qualify for a prize, but safe and unharmed.

People compete in the rodeo for different kinds of rewards. There are cash prizes that go to the winners. Sometimes the best all-around cowboy wins a horse trailer or a saddle. But I think the biggest reward is to perform well in front of the cheering crowds that fill the stadium.

One second...　　　　　　Two seconds...　　　　　　Three seconds...

Felecita uses a dummy steer with plastic horns to improve her roping skills.

The day after the rodeo ends, I am back on my horse and practicing again. I'm planning to ride in the rodeo next summer. If I try real hard, maybe I'll win a new saddle. But even without the saddle, it is always fun to compete in Whiteriver's Apache Rodeo.

GLOSSARY

Apache: (*ah-PAT-chee*) Tribe of Native Americans living in Arizona and New Mexico.

Apache bread: Flat bread, leavened with baking powder and baked over hot coals.

arbor: A harvest tipi for the Sunrise Ceremony made from four saplings.

Athapaskan: (*ATH-ah-PAS-kan*) Language family to which Apaches, Navajo, and some tribes in western Canada, Alaska, and the Pacific Coast belong.

bear grass: A tough, grassy plant used as thatch for Apache wickiups.

buckskin: Soft leather made from deer hide.

chaps: Leather coverings that cowboys and cowgirls strap onto their legs over their jeans to protect them while riding.

Chiricahua: (*CHI-rih-KOW-ah*) A band of Apaches now living in New Mexico and Oklahoma.

Crown Dancers: Representing the Mountain Spirits or G'aan, they wear black face masks and headdresses made of sotol slates. The dancers perform in healing and girls' "coming of age" ceremonies.

G'aan: Apache Mountain Spirits.

godmother: A woman who sponsors a girl in the Sunrise Ceremony and teaches her the traditional faith and way of living of the Apache people.

Jicarilla: (*hi-cah-REE-yah*) A band of Apaches now living in New Mexico.

kilt: A short buckskin skirt worn by the Crown Dancers.

Mescalero: (*mes-cah-LEH-roh*) A band of Apaches living in New Mexico. The name comes from the mescal or agave plants that the Apaches gather and roast for food.

Mountain Spirits: Supernatural beings or G'aan, whom Crown Dancers impersonate in Apache healing and "coming of age" rites.

piñon pitch: Sticky fluid from inside the piñon pine tree.

plateau: A high, flat area of land. Whiteriver is located on a plateau between the Mogollon Range of mountains to the north and the Salt River Canyon to the south.

Pueblo Indians: Groups of Native Americans that live in pueblos in the Southwestern United States.

ramada: (*rah-MAH-dah*) A frame in the shape of a rectangle made of poles. The roof is covered with brush for shading.

"rank" bull: A mean bull that is hard to ride.

reservation: A portion of land set aside by the U.S. government as a homeland for Native Americans.

rhombus stick: A special instrument made with a cord that has a block of wood on the end. The Crown Dancer called the "clown" swings it rapidly in a circle to create a loud, whirring sound like the wind.

rosin: A substance from the sap of a pine tree which, when rubbed onto a surface, makes it slightly sticky and easier to hold onto; used by cowboys on their bull ropes and bronc-riding equipment.

saddle soap: Liquid glycerine used for cleaning and conditioning leather saddles and tack.

sapling: The trunk of a young tree.

sotol: A cactus-like plant that grows near Whiteriver, Arizona. Lightweight and strong, sotol is used to make cradleboards and headdresses for the Crown Dancers.

sponsor: A person who takes charge of a girl's Sunrise Ceremony.

spurs: Devices with points worn on a rider's boots, used to grip the sides of a bull.

steers: Young male beef cattle.

stock: Short for livestock, meaning the broncos, bulls, and steers used in the rodeo.

stockman: A person who raises, trades for, and supplies stock, such as bulls, steers, and broncos, to the rodeo.

tule pollen: A powder found in the blossom of a plant in northeastern Arizona.

Western Apache: A group of Apaches that share the same language and culture and live in Arizona: the White Mountain Apache, Cibecue Apache, San Carlos Apache, Southern Tonto, and Northern Tonto.

wickiup: (*WIH-kee-up*) A traditional Apache home made from saplings and covered with grasses and brush.

INDEX

Page numbers in *italics* refer to illustrations.

APACHE INDIAN RESERVATIONS IN THE SOUTHWEST

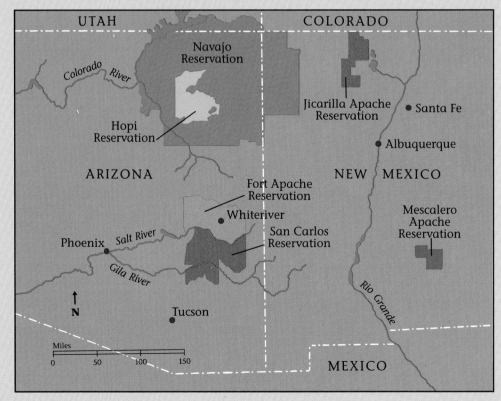